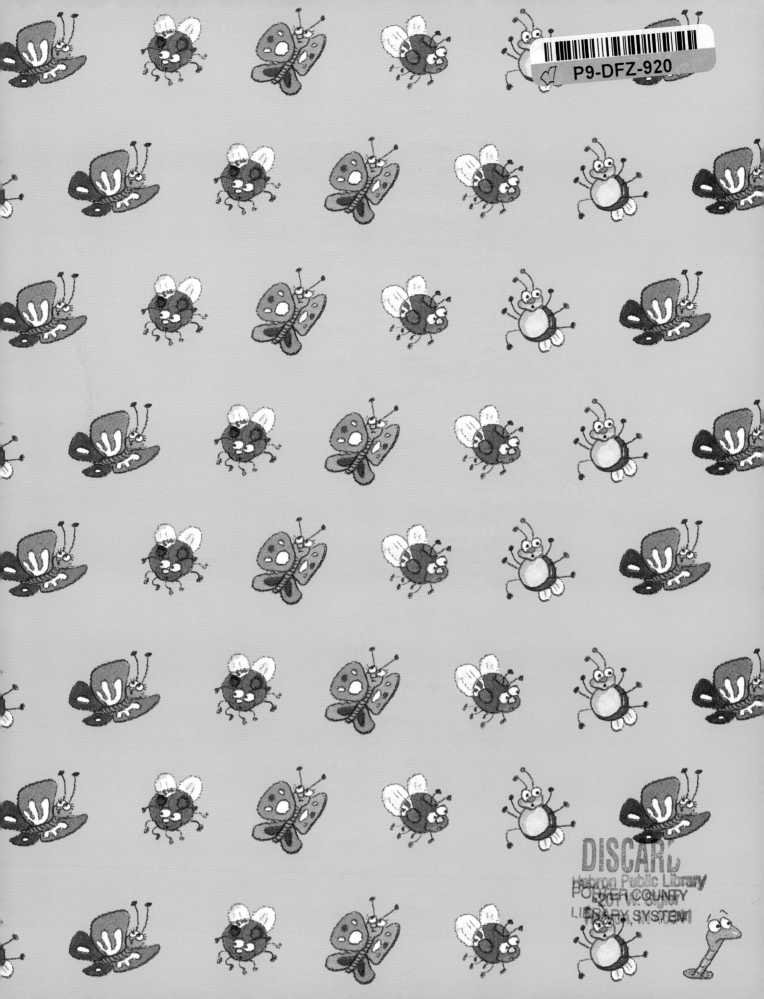

THE
BIG BAD
RUMOR

And this one's for Oliver—J.M.

For my brother Ben—J.E.

Text copyright © 2000 by Jonathan Meres
Illustrations copyright © 2000 by Jacqueline East
First American edition 2000 published by Orchard Books

First published in the United Kingdom in 2000 by
Hutchinson Children's Books, Random House UK Limited

Jonathan Meres and Jacqueline East assert their right to be identified
as the author and the illustrator of this work.

Orchard Books, A Grolier Company
95 Madison Avenue, New York, NY 10016

Manufactured in Singapore
The text of this book is set in 24 point Cheltenham Light.
The illustrations are watercolor.

1 3 5 7 9 10 8 6 4 2

Library of Congress Cataloging-in-Publication Data
Meres, Jonathan.
The big bad rumor / by Jonathan Meres ; illustrated by Jacqueline East.—
1st American ed.
p.   cm.
Summary: As the goggle-eyed goose's news about a wolf spreads from
animal to animal, the facts become monstrously distorted.
ISBN 0-531-30292-X (trade : alk. paper)
[1. Communication—Fiction. 2. Gossip—Fiction. 3. Animals—Fiction.]
I. East, Jacqueline, ill. II. Title.
PZ7.M5355 Bi 2000 [E]—dc21 99-89323

THE BIG BAD RUMOR

BY JONATHAN MERES
PICTURES BY JACQUELINE EAST

ORCHARD BOOKS

"There's a big bad wolf coming
and he's hopping mad!"
cried the goggle-eyed goose,
all in a flap.

"*What's that?* There's a hopping mad wolf and he's bad and he's big?" cried the whimpering weasel, whiskers twitching.

"*What's that?* There's a whopping bad wolf and he's wearing a wig?" cried the jittery jay, tail flicking.

"*What's that?* He's shopping mad and he's scaring a pig?" cried the harried hedgehog, prickles prickling.

"*What's that?* There's no stopping him now, he's so mean and scary?" cried the panicking polecat, body quivering.

"*What's that?* He's the size of a cow and incredibly hairy?" cried the muttering mole, nose dribbling.

NO, STOP!

"You've got it all wrong," cried the observant owl, eyes blazing. "Pay attention to Goose. Don't listen to Mole!"

"*What's that?* He wrestled a moose and then swallowed him whole?" cried the frantic fox, bushy tail bristling.

NO, NO!

"Quiet, everyone!" cried the goggle-eyed goose, in an even bigger flap. "This is becoming *ridiculous*!"

"*Who is?* Who's coming to tickle us?"
whispered the baffled beetle,
shell shivering.

"Stop! Stop! Stop!" cried the goggle-eyed goose,
in the biggest flap of all. "Now—listen . . .
very . . . carefully."

THERE'S A BIG BAD WOLF COMING AND HE'S HOPPING MAD!

"Yikes! That'll be him now! Quick, everyone, hide!"

Knock, knock!

"Who's there?"

"A small sad wolf…"

"A small sad wolf?"
"Are you hopping mad?"
"No..."

"You're not? Phew!"

"I'm a small sad wolf and…

...I'VE BROUGHT MY DAD!

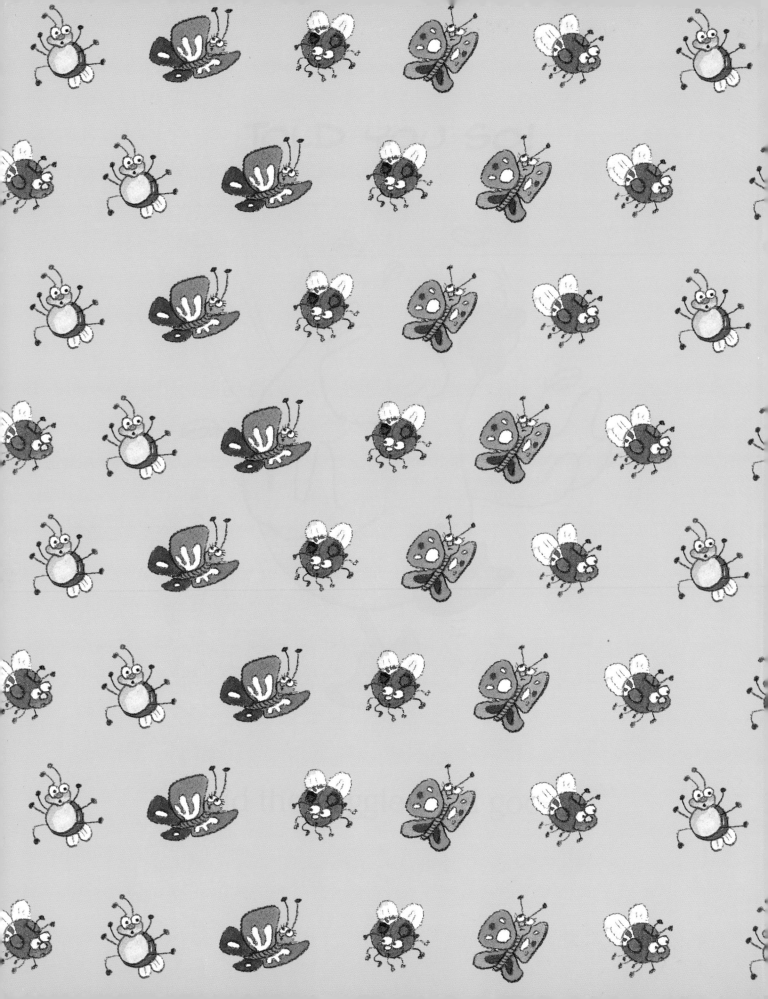